To Georg   —K.B.

Text copyright © 2007 by Kate Banks
Illustrations copyright © 2007 by Georg Hallensleben
All rights reserved
Distributed in Canada by Douglas & McIntyre Ltd.
Color separations by Chroma Graphics PTE Ltd.
Printed and bound in the United States of America by Phoenix Color Corporation
Designed by Barbara Grzeslo
First edition, 2007
10 9 8 7 6 5 4 3 2

www.fsgkidsbooks.com

Library of Congress Cataloging-in-Publication Data
Banks, Kate, date.
    Fox / Kate Banks ; pictures by Georg Hallensleben.— 1st ed.
        p.   cm.
    Summary: A baby fox anticipates the time when he can go out alone,
but first his parents must teach him the ways of the wilderness.
    ISBN-13: 978-0-374-39967-2
    ISBN-10: 0-374-39967-0
    1. Foxes—Juvenile fiction. [1. Foxes—Fiction.   2. Animals—Infancy—
Fiction.   3. Parental behavior in animals—Fiction.]   I. Hallensleben,
Georg, ill. II. Title.

PZ10.3.B2154Fox 2007
[E]—dc22
                                            2005047701

FOX

Kate Banks

**Pictures by
Georg Hallensleben**

Frances Foster Books

Farrar, Straus and Giroux   New York

It is spring.
In the forest, among the roots
of a great oak tree in a brown earthen den,
a baby fox is born.

And the rain comes and goes.
And the little stream grows into a rolling river.

The baby fox buries his head in his mama's thick fur,
the color of burnished leaves.
He sucks hungrily from her teat.

And the sun comes and goes.
And the buds start to show on the sprouting vines.

The little fox pokes his head out of the den.
He creeps toward the meadow.
"No, fox, no," says his mother.
"You're not ready," says his father.
"When will I be ready?" asks the little fox.

They wait until the sun sets,
bloated by the weight of day.
Then they lead the little fox out of the forest.
They leap like shadows through the fields.

And the stars come and go.
And the crescent moon grows into a big round ball.

The little fox is hungry.
His mama shows him how to find blackberries.
His father shows him how to catch rodents and birds.
"Am I ready?" the little fox asks.
"Not yet," says his mother.

And the clouds come and go.
And the small wind blows into a billowy gust.

The little fox pricks up his ears.
He hears a distant howling.
The enemy is nearby.
The little fox moves toward the sound.
"No, fox, no," says his papa.
He leads the little fox deeper into the forest,
far from danger.

And the sound comes and goes.
And the silence grows into a peaceable hum.

The little fox trots through the woods.
He watches his papa cross the river and he follows.
"No, fox, no," says his mother.
"When will I be ready?" asks the little fox.
"Soon," says his mother.

She shelters them in the shade of a tree.
Overhead, the branches sigh
like a lullaby setting the world at ease.

And the birds come and go.
And the saplings grow into tall, stately trees.

Fall comes.

The trees begin to shiver, and their leaves change color.

Mama gathers extra berries and seeds.

The little fox blinks his shiny eyes

and twitches his black velvet nose.

"Am I ready now?" he asks.

"Almost," says his mother.

His papa digs a shallow hole in the dirt
for storing food for the winter.
Then he retraces his footprints to mask his trail.

And the days come and go.
And the little fox grows strong and able.

At last, the little fox can hunt on his own.
He can feed himself and bury his food.
He can hide in the bushes and run like the wind.
"Now I'm ready," he says.
"Go, fox, go," says his mother.

And as the orange sun
leaves the sky, like a big goodbye,
the little fox goes.
And the mama fox knows
and the papa fox too
that he will be fine.